And then, in a twinkling, I heard on the roof,
The prancing and pawing of each little hoof—
As I drew in my head, and was turning around,
Down the chimney Saint Nicholas came with a bound.

He was dressed all in fur, from his head to his foot,
And his clothes were all tarnished with ashes and soot;
A bundle of toys he had flung on his back,
And he looked like a peddler just opening his pack.

His eyes—how they twinkled! His dimples, how merry!
His cheeks were like roses, his nose like a cherry!
His droll little mouth was drawn up like a bow,
And the beard of his chin was as white as the snow.

The stump of a pipe he held just in his teeth,
And the smoke, it encircled his head like a wreath;
He had a broad face and a little round belly
That shook when he laughed like a bowlful of jelly.

He was chubby and plump, a right jolly old elf,
And I laughed when I saw him, in spite of myself.
A wink of his eye and a twist of his head
Soon gave me to know I had nothing to dread.

He spoke not a word, but went straight to his work,
And filled all the stockings, then turned with a jerk,
And laying his finger aside of his nose,
And giving a nod, up the chimney he rose.

He sprang to his sleigh, to his team gave a whistle,
And away they all flew like the down of a thistle;
But I heard him exclaim, ere he drove out of sight,
"Happy Christmas to all, and to all a good night!"

—Clement Clarke Moore

The NIGHT BEFORE CHRISTMAS

Can You See What I See?

The Night Before Christmas

PICTURE PUZZLES TO SEARCH AND SOLVE

by Walter Wick

SCHOLASTIC INC.

New York Toronto London Auckland Sydney

Mexico City New Delhi Hong Kong Buenos Aires

Published by Scholastic Inc.

SCHOLASTIC, CARTWHEEL BOOKS, and

associated logos are trademarks and/or

registered trademarks of Scholastic Inc.

ISBN–13: 978-0-439-76927-3

ISBN–10: 0-439-76927-2

20 19 18 17 16 15 14 13 14 15 16

Printed in Malaysia 108

First printing, September 2005

Book Design by Walter Wick and David Saylor

For my mother, Betty Wick, with love,

—W.W.

Library of Congress Cataloging-in-Publication Data

Wick, Walter.

Can you see what I see? The night before Christmas : picture puzzles to search

and solve / by Walter Wick. p. cm.

"Cartwheel books."

ISBN 0-439-76927-2 (hardcover)

1. Picture puzzles--Juvenile literature. 2. Children's poetry, American. 3. Santa

Claus--Juvenile poetry. 4. Christmas--Juvenile poetry. I. Title: Night before Christ-

mas. II. Moore, Clement Clarke, 1779-1863. Night before Christmas. III. Title.

GV1507.P47W514 2005

793.73--dc22 2005005644

CONTENTS

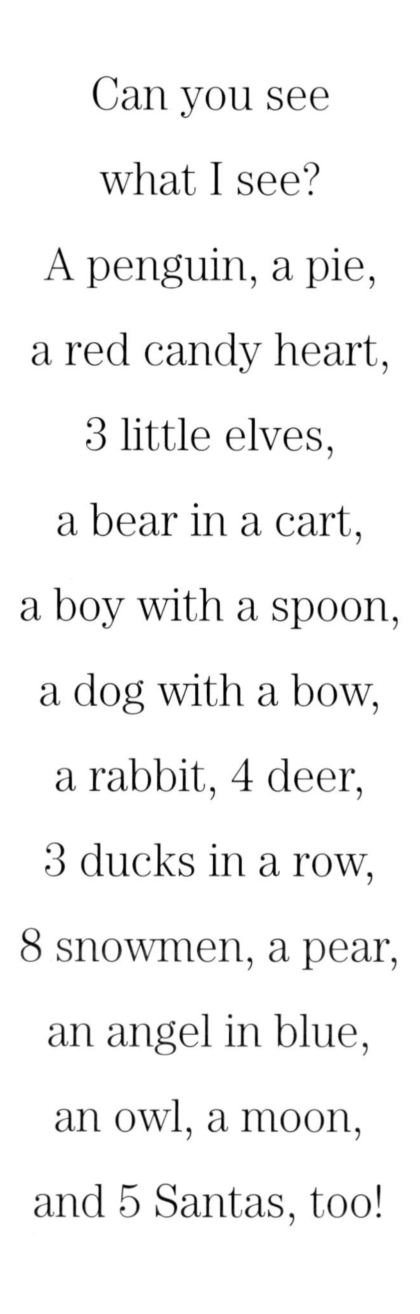

Can you see
what I see?
A penguin, a pie,
a red candy heart,
3 little elves,
a bear in a cart,
a boy with a spoon,
a dog with a bow,
a rabbit, 4 deer,
3 ducks in a row,
8 snowmen, a pear,
an angel in blue,
an owl, a moon,
and 5 Santas, too!

NOT A CREATURE WAS STIRRING

Can you see
what I see?
A monkey, 5 elves,
a train, 2 wagons,
a duck, 6 horses,
an ace, 2 dragons,
a turkey, a rooster,
a whistle, 2 clocks,
a Christmas greeting
spelled out on blocks,
11 snowflakes,
7 white sheep,
a giraffe afloat,
and a mouse asleep!

STEVEN
STORE
C1350

THE STOCKINGS

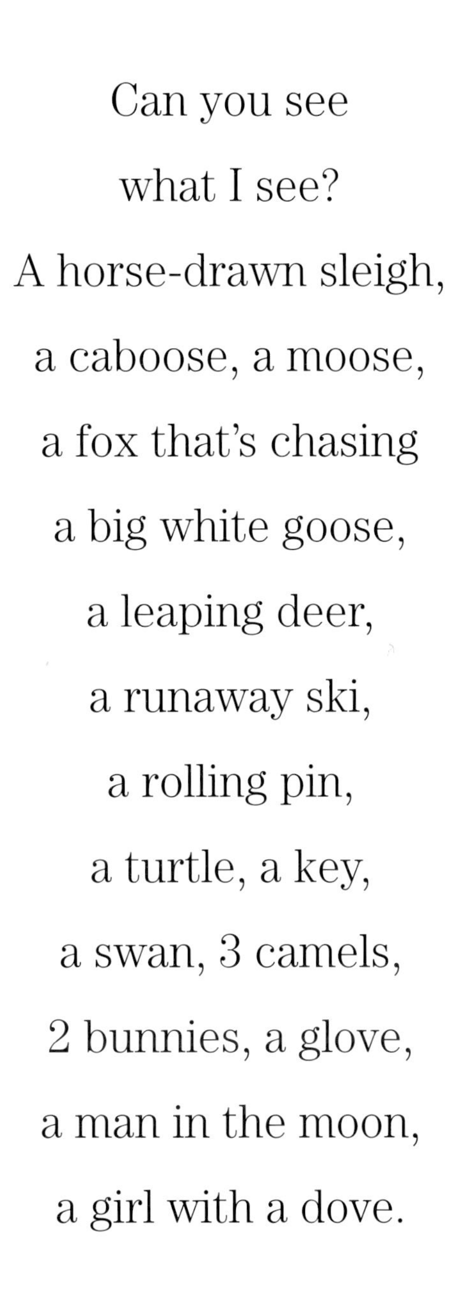

Can you see
what I see?
A horse-drawn sleigh,
a caboose, a moose,
a fox that's chasing
a big white goose,
a leaping deer,
a runaway ski,
a rolling pin,
a turtle, a key,
a swan, 3 camels,
2 bunnies, a glove,
a man in the moon,
a girl with a dove.

ALL SNUG

Can you see
what I see?
A clock, 2 scissors,
Santa with a sack,
a silver flashlight,
a red thumbtack,
a dino, a deer,
a thimble, an ace,
NOEL, 3 elephants,
a blue shoelace,
2 spools for stools,
a button that's red,
a bunny, 2 bears,
all snug in their bed!

NOEL

VISIONS OF SUGARPLUMS

Can you see
what I see?
A gingerbread house,
a spoon on a dish,
a carriage, a cork,
a chicken, 5 fish,
a basket of fruit,
a peanut, a pocket,
an ice-cream cone,
a robot, a rocket,
a sweet blue angel,
a teapot, a plane,
3 sugarplums,
and a candy train!

A LONG WINTER'S NAP

Can you see
what I see?
A partridge, 3 geese,
a camel, 2 cars,
a key, a clothespin,
a cradle, 5 stars,
a candle, 3 hearts,
a donkey, a calf,
a toothbrush, 2 books,
5 bells, a giraffe,
a polka-dot kerchief,
a blue shoelace,
a plane, and a map
to a very cool place.

SUCH A CLATTER!

Can you see
what I see?
A bell, 2 drummers,
a windup dog,
a ballerina,
a noisy frog,
a saw, a trumpet,
a teapot, a sled,
a shoe that's blue,
a barn that's red,
2 polar bears,
a little fawn,
a snowman on
a snowy lawn!

NEW FALLEN SNOW

Can you see
what I see?
3 downy feathers,
8 birds, a kitten,
a skater, 2 skis,
a yellow mitten,
a ring, a tiger,
a wreath, a tassel,
the eye of a needle,
a king, a castle,
a shoe for a horse,
a button that's clear,
a miniature sleigh,
and 8 tiny reindeer!

DOWN THE CHIMNEY

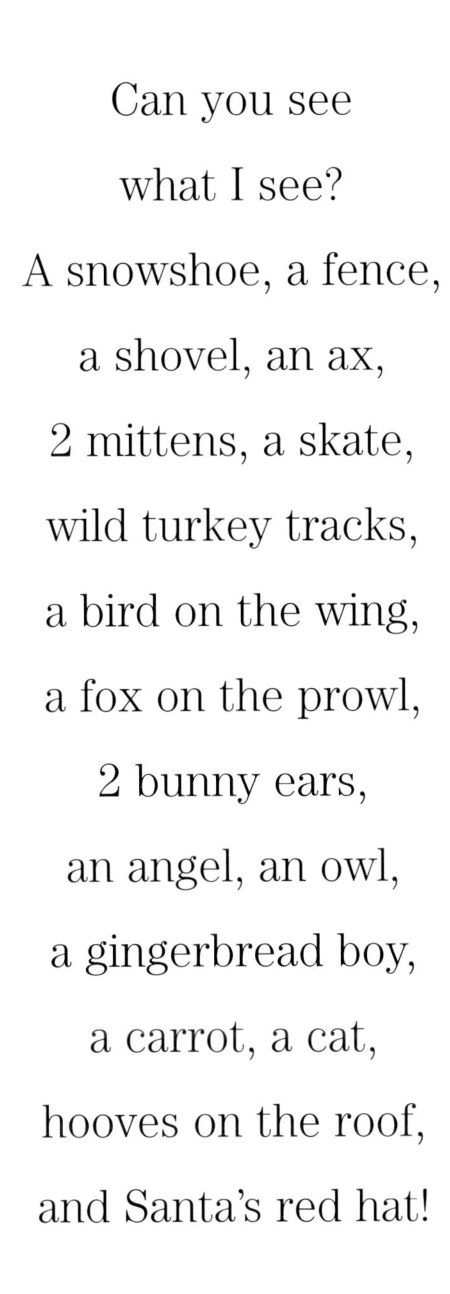

Can you see
what I see?
A snowshoe, a fence,
a shovel, an ax,
2 mittens, a skate,
wild turkey tracks,
a bird on the wing,
a fox on the prowl,
2 bunny ears,
an angel, an owl,
a gingerbread boy,
a carrot, a cat,
hooves on the roof,
and Santa's red hat!

IT MUST BE SAINT NICK

Can you see
what I see?
A rooster, a swan,
a rabbit, 3 bears,
a button, a bat,
a pinecone, 2 pears,
a bell, a trumpet,
a grandfather clock,
a bird that is blue,
a heart on a block,
3 candle flames,
a wooden matchstick,
boots, and the shadow
of old Saint Nick!

A BUNDLE OF TOYS

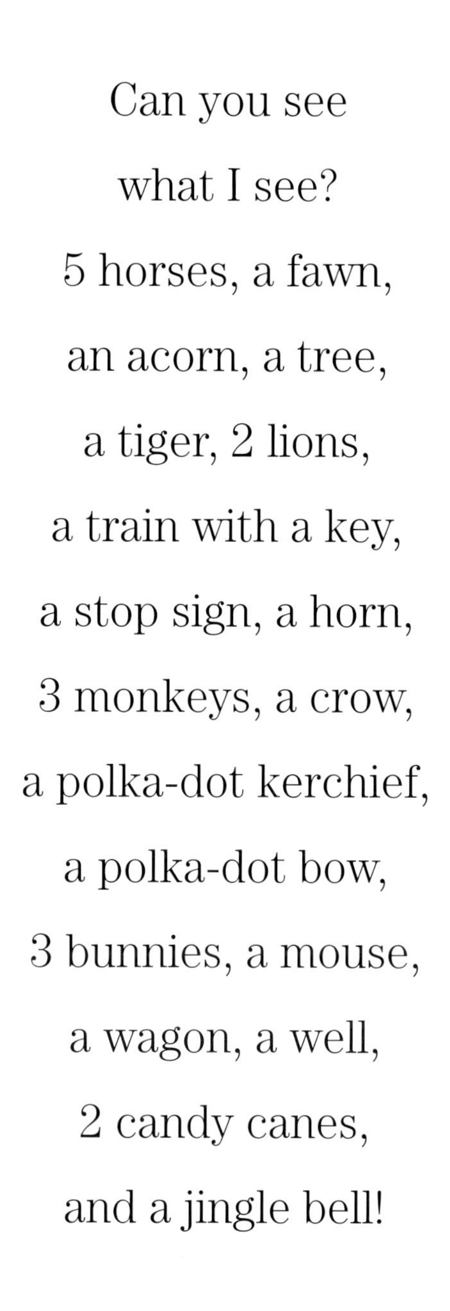

Can you see
what I see?
5 horses, a fawn,
an acorn, a tree,
a tiger, 2 lions,
a train with a key,
a stop sign, a horn,
3 monkeys, a crow,
a polka-dot kerchief,
a polka-dot bow,
3 bunnies, a mouse,
a wagon, a well,
2 candy canes,
and a jingle bell!

HAPPY CHRISTMAS TO ALL!

Can you see
what I see?
An angel, a feather,
2 cookie trees,
an owl, a swan,
a skier on skis,
a train, 2 snowmen,
3 bunnies, a mouse,
a gumdrop, a spoon,
a gingerbread house,
a Christmas tree
with a star so bright,
and Santa waving
to all a good night!

The world of children's literature presents unique challenges to the photographic illustrator. In the realm of the written word and hand-drawn illustrations, skilled writers and artists can evoke imaginary worlds and conjure wild flights of fancy. The photographer's realm is, however, based in reality. Wondrous events like those depicted in Clement Clarke Moore's 1823 poem originally titled "A Visit from Saint Nicholas" are not readily available to even the most resourceful photographer, and reenacting such events is not without its difficulties, since reindeer are generally unaccustomed to taking direction from anyone, with the exception, perhaps, of Saint Nicholas himself. And as to the availability of that "jolly old elf," well, let's just say he's a very busy man.

Given the inherent limitations of this reality-based medium, I decided to adapt the time-honored classic, now known as "The Night Before Christmas," as a search-and-find game using photographs of Christmas decorations both old and new; Christmas cookies, candies, and other treats; handmade props and sets; and of course, a mountain of toys. All real objects, but alas, no real reindeer.

And while "old Saint Nick" is more elusive here than in most illustrated versions of the story, it's my hope that young readers will find him present in spirit, and it's my expectation that readers, gifted as they are with the power of observation and adept as they are in the realm of the imagination, will freely improvise their own interpretations of the photographs.

Acknowledgments
I created and photographed all the sets in my studio with the help of a dedicated team of staff members and freelance artists. I'm deeply indebted to all on the team for their many contributions to this book: to studio manager Dan Helt, whose wide-ranging technical expertise was invaluable in the photography studio, the computer lab, and the workshop; to prop manager Kim Wildey, who, amid much chaos, could locate any prop at any time, all while accomplishing numerous other organizational and artistic tasks; to artist Michael Lokensgaard, who made many detailed and beautifully painted props, including the house facade in "It Must Be Saint Nick," the mantle and snow scene in "The Stockings," the snow globe base in "New Fallen Snow," the cardboard house in "All Snug," and the shelf in "Not a Creature Was Stirring;" to artist Randy Gilman, who made equally beautiful and meticulously crafted props, including the house featured on the cover and in "Down the Chimney," the ornament houses in "Happy Christmas to All," the stockings that hang from the mantle in "The Stockings," Santa's bag in "A Bundle of Toys," the handcrafted Santa sleigh on this page, and many other whimsical accessories; to artist Mike Dunne, who provided valuable assistance in the construction and painting of props, including the fine airbrush work on Seymour's horse (this page); to food stylist Rick Ellis, who labored three long days in the kitchen, where he baked and decorated the gingerbread house and all the Christmas cookies; to Rick Schwab, for three hours of the most valuable PhotoShop lessons I've ever had; to Sandy at A Special Place, for floral advice and props; and finally, a very special thanks to my wife, Linda, for not only helping to put this team together, but for keeping it together, for her expert propping advice, and as always, for her infinite artistic wisdom.

At Scholastic, I'm eternally grateful to my editor Grace Maccarone for her patience during my many missteps and false starts leading up to this project and for her expert guidance that ultimately led to the book you now hold in your hand; to editorial director Ken Geist for his generous enthusiasm and support; to creative director David Saylor for his excellent advice on this project; to art director Stephen Hughes for his creative design contributions; to publicist Clare McMahon for her diligence and good cheer; and to Barbara Marcus and Jean Feiwel for keeping the faith! –Walter Wick

All sets were designed, arranged, photographed, and photo retouched by the author. Photographs were taken with a Sinar P3 Camera equipped with a Sinar 54 (22 mega pixel) digital back. Photo retouching was done on Apple Computers using Adobe PhotoShop editing software.

Walter Wick is the photographer of the I Spy series of books, with more than twenty-four million copies in print. He is author and photographer of *A Drop of Water: A Book of Science and Wonder*, which won the Boston Globe/Horn Book Award for Nonfiction, was named a Notable Children's Book by the American Library Association, and was selected as an Orbis Pictus Honor Book and a CBC/NSTA Outstanding Science Trade Book for Children. *Walter Wick's Optical Tricks*, a book of photographic illusions, was named a Best Illustrated Children's Book by the *New York Times Book Review*, was recognized as a Notable Children's Book by the American Library Association, and received many awards, including a Platinum Award from the Oppenheim Toy Portfolio, a Young Readers Award from *Scientific American*, a *Bulletin* Blue Ribbon, and a Parents' Choice Silver Honor. *Can You See What I See?*, published in 2003, appeared on the *New York Times* Bestseller List for twenty-two weeks. His most recent books in the Can You See What I See? series are *Dream Machine*, *Seymour and the Juice Box Boat*, and *Cool Collections*. Mr. Wick has invented photographic games for *GAMES* magazine and photographed covers for books and magazines, including *Newsweek, Discover*, and *Psychology Today*. A graduate of Paier College of Art, Mr. Wick lives in Connecticut with his wife, Linda.

A Visit from Saint Nicholas

'Twas the night before Christmas, when all through the house,
Not a creature was stirring, not even a mouse;
The stockings were hung by the chimney with care,
In hopes that Saint Nicholas soon would be there;

The children were nestled all snug in their beds,
While visions of sugarplums danced in their heads.
And Mama in her kerchief, and I in my cap,
Had just settled our brains for a long winter's nap—

When out on the lawn there arose such a clatter,
I sprang from the bed to see what was the matter.
Away to the window I flew like a flash,
Tore open the shutters, and threw up the sash.

The moon on the breast of the new fallen snow
Gave the luster of midday to objects below;
When, what to my wondering eyes should appear,
But a miniature sleigh, and eight tiny reindeer,

With a little old driver, so lively and quick,
I knew in a moment it must be Saint Nick.
More rapid than eagles, his coursers they came,
And he whistled, and shouted, and called them by name:

"Now, DASHER! Now, DANCER! Now, PRANCER! Now, VIXEN!
On, COMET! On, CUPID! On, DONDER and BLITZEN!
To the top of the porch! To the top of the wall!
Now dash away! Dash away! Dash away, all!"

As dry leaves that before the wild hurricane fly,
When they meet with an obstacle, mount to the sky;
So up to the house-top the coursers they flew,
With the sleigh full of toys—and Saint Nicholas, too.